CHANTICLEER AND THE FOX · BY GEOFFREY CHAUCER

Chanticleer
AND THE FOX

BY GEOFFREY CHAUCER

ADAPTED AND ILLUSTRATED

BY BARBARA COONEY

THOMAS Y. CROWELL COMPANY

NEW YORK

This adaptation of the "Nun's Priest's Tale" from *The Canterbury Tales*, translated by Robert Mayer Lumiansky, is used with the kind permission of Simon & Schuster, Inc., copyright 1948 by Simon & Schuster, Inc.

Chanticleer and the Fox

Library of Congress Catalog Card Number: 58-10449
ISBN 0-690-18561-8
ISBN 0-690-18562-6 (lib. bdg.)
ISBN 0-06-443087-1 (pbk.)

Published in hardcover by Thomas Y. Crowell, New York.
First Harper Trophy edition, 1989.

nce upon a time a poor widow, getting
on in years, lived in a small cottage beside a grove which stood in a little valley. This
widow, about whom I shall tell you my tale, had
patiently led a very simple life since the day her
husband died. By careful management she was able
to take care of herself and her two daughters.

She had only three large sows, three cows, and also a sheep called Molly.

Her bedroom was very sooty, as was her kitch-
en in which she ate many a scanty meal. She was
never sick from overeating. Her table was usually set
with only white and black—milk and dark bread, of
which there was no shortage—and sometimes there
was broiled bacon and an egg or two, for she was,
as it were, a kind of dairywoman.

She had a yard, fenced all around with sticks, in which she had a rooster named Chanticleer. For crowing there was not his equal in all the land. His voice was merrier than the merry organ that plays in church, and his crowing from his resting place was more trustworthy than a clock. His comb was redder than fine coral and turreted like a castle wall, his bill was black and shone like jet, and his legs and toes were like azure. His nails were whiter than the lily, and his feathers were like burnished gold.

Now this fine rooster had seven hens, all col-
ored exceedingly like him. The hen with the pret-
tiest throat was called fair Demoiselle Partlet. She
was polite, discreet, debonair, and companionable,
and she had conducted herself so well since the time

that she was seven days old that, truly, she held the
heart of Chanticleer all tightly locked. It was a great
joy to hear them sing in sweet harmony when the
bright sun began to rise. For in those days, so I'm
told, beasts and birds could talk and sing.

And so it happened, one day at dawn, as Chanticleer sat on his perch surrounded by the hens, that he began to groan in his throat like a man troubled by his dreams. When Partlet heard him moaning this way she was frightened and said: "Dear heart, what ails you that you groan in such a manner?"

And he answered saying: "Madam, I dreamed just now that I was in much danger. I dreamed that I was roaming up and down within our yard, when I saw a beast like a hound which tried to grab my body and would have killed me. His color was between yellow and red, and his tail and both ears were tipped with black, different from the rest of his fur. His snout was small and his two eyes glowed. I almost died of fear at the sight of him; doubtless that's what caused my groaning."

"Go on!" she said. "Shame on you, you know I cannot love a coward, by my faith! Haven't you a man's heart and haven't you a beard? Be merry, husband. Do not fear dreams."

"Thank you, Madam Partlet," he said, "for your learned advice. I do say that when I see the beauty of your face all scarlet red about the eyes, my fears die away."

And with these words he flew down from the rafter, along with all the hens, for it was day. With a clucking he called them all to some grain which he found lying about the yard. He was as regal as a prince in his palace and was no longer afraid. He looked like a lion as he roamed up and down on his toes; he barely set foot to the earth.

Chanticleer, walking in all his pride, with his seven wives beside him, cast up his eyes at the bright sun. He crowed with a happy voice, "Listen how the happy birds sing, and how the fresh flowers grow; my heart is full of gaiety and joy."

But suddenly a sorrowful event overtook him.

A fox, tipped with black, and full of sly wickedness, had lived in the grove three years. That same night he burst through the hedges into the yard where fair Chanticleer and his wives were in the habit of going. And this fox lay quietly in a bed of herbs until almost noon of that day.

Partlet, with all her sisters nearby, lay merrily bathing in the sand, with her back to the sun, and the lordly Chanticleer sang more joyfully than the mermaid in the sea.

Now it happened that, as he cast his eye upon a butterfly among the herbs, Chanticleer became aware of the fox lying low. He had no desire to crow then, but at once cried, "Cok! cok!" and started up like a man frightened in his heart.

And he would have fled at once, if the fox had not said: "My dear sir, alas, where are you going? Are you afraid of me, your father's friend? The reason I came was only to listen to you sing. For, truly, you have as merry a voice as any angel in heaven. My lord your father—God bless his soul—and also your courteous mother did me the great honor of visiting my house. Except for you I have never heard anyone who could sing as your father did in the morning. In order to make his voice stronger, he would close both his eyes. And he would stand on his tiptoes and stretch forth his long slender neck. Now sing, sir, for holy charity; let's see whether you can sing as well as your father."

Chanticleer began to beat his wings. He stood high on his toes and stretched his neck, closed his eyes, and crowed loudly. At once the fox jumped up, grabbed Chanticleer by the throat, and carried him toward the woods.

Alas, that Chanticleer flew down from the rafters! Alas, that his wife took no heed of dreams! And all this trouble came on a Friday.

Such a cry was never made as was made by all the hens in the yard when they saw Chanticleer captured. The poor widow and her two daughters heard the woeful cries of the hens and at once ran out of doors. They saw the fox going toward the grove, carrying away the rooster. "Help! Help! Woe is me! Look, a fox!" they screamed, and ran after him.

The cows, the sheep, and even the hogs, so frightened were they by the shouting, ran after him, too. They ran so hard they thought their hearts would burst.

The neighbors' ducks quacked as if they were to be killed; and their geese, from fear, flew over the trees; the noise was so terrible that the bees swarmed from their hive. It seemed that heaven would fall.

Now, good people, I beg you all to listen. This rooster in the fox's mouth spoke to the fox in spite of his fear, saying, ''Sir, if I were you, so help me God, I would say, 'Turn back, you proud peasants! I have reached the edge of the wood now; the rooster shall stay here. In spite of you I will eat him, in faith, and not be long about it.' ''

"In faith," the fox answered, "it shall be done." As soon as he spoke the words, the rooster nimbly broke away from his mouth and flew at once high into a tree.

When the fox saw that the rooster was gone, he said, "Alas! Oh, Chanticleer, alas! I have done you a bad turn. I frightened you when I grabbed you and took you out of the yard. But, sir, I did it without evil intention. Come down and I shall tell you what I meant."

"Nay, then," said Chanticleer. "Never again shall you with your flattery get me to sing with my eyes closed. For he who closes his eyes when he should watch, God let him never prosper."

"No," said the fox, "but God bring misfortune to him who is so careless about his self-control as to prattle when he should hold his peace."

"See," said the widow as the fox slunk into the grove, "that is the result of trusting in flattery."

And she marched with her flock back to the yard in the little valley.